MY PHOTOGRAPH ALBUM

A BEATRIX POTTER KEEPSAKE

Devised and compiled by Frances Brace

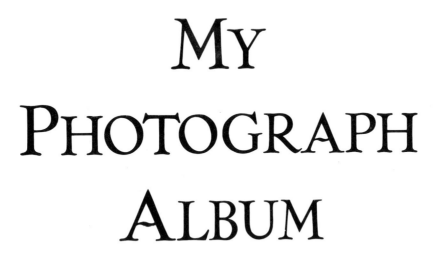

With new reproductions from the original illustrations by
BEATRIX POTTER

F. WARNE & Co. ™

Beatrix Potter, whose familiar characters decorate these pages,
was a keen photographer, and her father Rupert Potter was so expert
that he used to take photographs for use as reference by famous
painters of his day. He took this picture of Beatrix and
her brother Bertram when Beatrix was twelve.

FREDERICK WARNE

Published by the Penguin Group
27 Wrights Lane, London W8 5TZ, England
Viking Penguin Inc., 40 West 23rd Street, New York, New York 10010, USA
Penguin Books Australia Ltd, Ringwood, Victoria, Australia
Penguin Books Canada Ltd, 2801 John Street, Markham, Ontario, Canada L3R 1B4
Penguin Books (NZ) Ltd, 182–190 Wairau Road, Auckland 10, New Zealand

Penguin Books Ltd, Registered Offices: Harmondsworth, Middlesex, England

First published 1988

Text copyright © Frances Brace, 1988

ISBN 0 7232 3514 7

Typeset by Rowland Phototypesetting (London) Ltd

Printed and bound in Great Britain by William Clowes Limited,
Beccles and London

INSTRUCTIONS

Here is your very own photograph album. It gives you the chance to arrange your photographs in the most imaginative and attractive way.

•

Choose a photograph for each page. You may already have a suitable photograph or you may want to take a picture especially for it.

•

Decide what you would like to write about the photograph. You may want to copy some of the suggested words and phrases, but use your own ideas wherever you can.

•

Stick or glue the photograph on the page using a non-solvent-based glue or special mounts. Make sure that the picture hides the list of 'Words you may like to use'. If necessary, trim your picture so that it fits neatly on the page.

•

When you have filled in all the sections you will find three pages at the end of the book where you can put extra photographs and captions on any subject of your choice.

•

If you have an enlarged photograph of yourself, your family or an important occasion, you can complete the album by mounting it here to cover these instructions. It will then form the first page of a book all about you and your own life, which you can keep for yourself or give to a very special friend or relative.

Words you may like to use
my mother
my father
a monkey
a prince
a princess
a frog
a doll

From *The Tale of The Flopsy Bunnies*

My name is ....

When I was a baby I looked just like ....

· ME ·

Words you may like to use

blond   blue
brown   brown
black   grey
red   green

          smart
          pretty
          angelic
          naughty
          sad

My birthday is ....

My hair is .... and my eyes are ....

Here I am looking ....

From *The Tale of Timmy Tiptoes*

· MY FAMILY ·

Here is Benjamin Bunny's family tree:

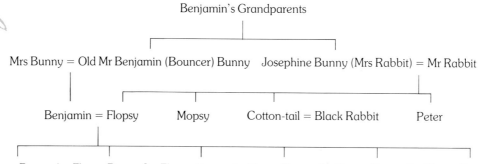

Benjamin's Grandparents

Mrs Bunny = Old Mr Benjamin (Bouncer) Bunny   Josephine Bunny (Mrs Rabbit) = Mr Rabbit

Benjamin = Flopsy   Mopsy   Cotton-tail = Black Rabbit   Peter

Flopsy Bunny 1   Flopsy Bunny 2   Flopsy Bunny 3   Flopsy Bunny 4   Flopsy Bunny 5   Flopsy Bunny 6

Here is my family tree:

From *The Tale of The Flopsy Bunnies*

· MY FAMILY ·

Words you may like to use

my mother	my father
mummy	daddy
mommy	dad
mum	papa
mom	
mama	

This is a photograph of ....

From *The Tale of Peter Rabbit*

· MY FAMILY ·

Words you may like to use
brother
step-brother
sister
half-sister
cousin
aunt
uncle

From *The Tale of Peter Rabbit*

Here is my ....

....

· MY FAMILY ·

Words you may like to use
grandmother
granny
grandma
grandfather
grandad
grandpa
godparents

This picture shows ....

From *The Tale of The Flopsy Bunnies*

From *The Tale of Peter Rabbit*

From *The Tale of Mr. Jeremy Fisher*

From *The Tale of Timmy Tiptoes*

From *The Tale of Johnny Town-Mouse*

· MY HOME ·

My address is ....

....

....

I live in a ....

Words you may like to use
house
flat
apartment
castle
hotel
bungalow
cottage

· MY FRIENDS ·

Words you may like to use
at the park
in the garden
in the street
in town
in the country
in school

From *The Tale of Mr. Jeremy Fisher*

My friends are called ....

....

We like to spend our time ....

·MY FRIENDS·

Words you may like to use
playing
drawing and painting
laughing and giggling
fighting
dancing
reading

From *The Tale of Johnny Town-Mouse*

What we enjoy most is

· GAMES ·

Words you may like to use
catch
tag
football
dressing up
computer games
hide-and-seek
pillow fights

The games I like best are ....

....

From *The Tale of Tom Kitten*

Words you may like to use
after school
in the playground
outside
when we should be in bed
quietly
noisily

We play ....

....

From *Peter Rabbit's Almanac for 1929*

From *The Tale of Tom Kitten*

From *The Tale of Benjamin Bunny*

From *Appley Dapply's Nursery Rhymes*

From *The Tale of The Flopsy Bunnies*

· DRESSING UP ·

When I wore this outfit I was ....

....

But I most like wearing ....

·SPECIAL OCCASIONS·

Words you may like to use
Christmas
Ramadan
Hanukkah
Thanksgiving
New Year
wedding
birthday

From *The Tale of Mrs. Tittlemouse*

Here we are celebrating ....

Words you may like to use
decorated the room
prepared the food
danced
sang
laughed
ate and drank

From *The Tale of Mrs. Tittlemouse*

On that day we ....

....

At this ....

the guests were ....

....

....

....

....

....

The games we played were ....

....

....

....

....

The best party foods are ....

....

From *The Tale of Johnny Town-Mouse*

·MY PARTY·

Words you may like to use

birthday party   sandwiches
tea party   crisps
dinner party   ice-cream
school party   cake
picnic   chips

•

musical chairs
pass the parcel
hunt the thimble

From *The Tale of Johnny Town-Mouse*

·OUR DAY OUT·

Words you may like to use

the lake

the sea

the country

the park

the mountains

the zoo

the museum

On

we went to

·OUR DAY OUT·

Words you may like to use
playing
looking at things
collecting
having a picnic
getting wet
fishing
walking

We spent the day ....

From *The Tale of Mr. Jeremy Fisher*

·OUR HOLIDAY·

Some of the things you may want to tell

Who did you go with?

How did you travel?

Where did you go?

Where did you stay?

Who did you meet?

What did you enjoy most?

What didn't you like?

From *The Tale of Pigling Bland*

This is what we did

....

....

·OUR HOLIDAY·

Words you may like to use

vacation	stayed up late
boat	visited interesting
plane	places
train	adventure
bus	climbing
tent	exploring
hotel	swimming
farmhouse	beach

....

....

....

From *The Tale of Johnny Town-Mouse*

·WATER·

Words you may like to use

bath-time

swimming

on a boat

in the rain

paddling

washing up

washing the car

From *The Tale of Tom Kitten*

This photograph shows ....

....

....

·ACTION·

Words you may like to use
me dancing
us running
skipping
hopping
swinging
walking
crawling

Here you can see ....

....

....

From *The Tale of Jemima Puddle-Duck*

Words you may like to use

bus

car

boat

bike

skis

skateboard

roller skates

plane

train

From *The Tale of Squirrel Nutkin*

I like to travel by . . . .

·ANIMALS·

The animal I like best is ....

What I like about it is ....

....

From *The Tale of Mrs. Tiggy-Winkle*

From *The Tale of Peter Rabbit*

From *The Tale of Jemima Puddle-Duck*

From *The Tailor of Gloucester*